Babar characters TM & © 1990 L. de Brunhoff
All rights reserved
Based on the animated series "Babar"
A Nelvana-Ellipse Presentation
a Nelvana Production in Association with The Clifford Ross Company, Ltd

Based on characters created by Jean and Laurent de Brunhoff

Based on a story by Peter Sauder
Image adaptation by Van Gool-Lefèvre-Loiseaux
Produced by Twin Books U.K. Ltd, London

This 1990 edition published by JellyBean Press,
distributed by Outlet Book Company, Inc.,
a Random House Company,
225 Park Avenue South
New York NY 10003

ISBN 0-517-052075

8 7 6 5 4 3 2 1

Printed and bound in Barcelona, Spain by Cronion, S.A.

BABAR

An Elephant's Best Friend

JellyBean Press
New York

Poor Flora. Her goldfish had died, and she was crying over the empty bowl, as Babar tried to comfort her.

"I know," he said. "It's very hard to say goodbye to something you love. When I was a little king, I had a very dear pet named Reginald—a baby warthog...

"...It all began when Rataxes, the rhinoceros king, set up a blockade to take away all our pomegranates. Of course, this fruit is very important to our economy, so there was a big demonstration outside the palace. All the elephants were waving signs and chanting, "We want our pomegranates! We want our pomegranates!"

Pompadour advised Babar to make peace with Rataxes, so that everyone would be happy again. So did General Cornelius. But Babar did not agree.

"Why should we make peace with Rataxes?" asked Babar. "That would be like rewarding him for stealing from us! Then he will blockade something else we need. No deals! Once you give in to a bully, it never ends."

At the palace of Rataxes, Basil was giving his master a full report on the pomegranate crisis in Celesteville. "Babar's subjects are very angry," he said. "Without their pomegranates, they can't make salads, jellies, or fruit punch. Fruit sellers are going out of business."

"Excellent," said Rataxes, gazing at the heaps of pomegranates all around him. "Babar will have to come crawling to me."

Just then, Rataxes heard the unmistakable sound of his wife's voice. "Ra-*tax*-es!" she bellowed in a loud singsong. "It's time for Reginald to take his *waa-alk*!"

"Oh, no!" groaned Rataxes, as a half-grown warthog charged him with bared teeth and tusks. Rataxes leaped off his throne and tried to climb the wall before the warthog could take a bite out of his dress uniform—or out of him!

"Now, now," scolded Lady Rataxes, recapturing her pet. "I wish you two would get along." She pushed the growling warthog into Rataxes' arms.

"Why don't *you* walk him?" demanded Rataxes.

"But this is your chance to be Reggie's *friend*," cooed Lady Rataxes.

"Basil!" shouted Rataxes, as
Reginald dragged him outside.
"Where are you, you blockhead?"
"Coming, Your Highness!"
cried Basil.

Once Basil got Reginald under control, Rataxes was free to make a plan for getting rid of the warthog, who was trying to trip him up at every step.

"This is ridiculous," fumed Rataxes. "The only thing to do is to leave him here in the jungle. But what will I tell my wife?"

"I've got it!" said Basil. "You were playing with the little pest—I mean, pet—and he broke his leash and ran away."

"Brilliant!" said Rataxes.

Basil unhooked Reggie's leash and picked up a stick. "Fetch!" he yelled, throwing it as far as he could.

With a look of delight, Reggie sprang away after the stick and disappeared among the trees.

When Reggie found the stick, he bounded back to the clearing—only to find it empty. Grunting loudly, he began to search for Basil and Rataxes. Just the thought of being lost in the jungle was already making him weak with hunger.

Luckily, the little warthog finally wandered into Babar's garden. "Well, hello!" said Babar (glad of any excuse to stop worrying about pomegranates). "What a cute little fellow! Are you lost? We shall be friends!"

Reggie had found a new home.

Meanwhile, Rataxes had gone nervously into his wife's sitting room to tell her that Reggie was gone. Lady Rataxes collapsed into hysterics.

"My Reggie!" she wailed. "My dear little warthog! How could you let him get lost in the jungle? It only shows how little you love me!"

"Now, now, my dear"—sputtered Rataxes. "Please don't distress yourself. Somehow, I'll get the little brute—ah, darling—back."

"*That's* the dear husband I married," sobbed Lady Rataxes.

Meanwhile, Babar and Reggie were playing happily in the garden. "How nice it is to have a pet," thought Babar. "And it keeps me out of those tiresome meetings about pomegranates."

Just then, Pompadour poked his elegant wig out of the window, and Babar sighed. "All we need is your seal of approval on the agreement with Rataxes, Sire," called the prime minister. None of them noticed that two strange bushes had appeared in the garden—bushes with feet!

Suddenly, Reggie caught the scent of Rataxes and sped toward the larger bush. Crunch! Another bite out of Rataxes and his dress uniform!

"Yikes!" yelled Rataxes, sticking his head out of the bush. He ran toward the palace, with Basil close behind. Reggie and Babar chased the bushes onto the balcony, where they disappeared.

"Guards!" called Babar.
"Come quickly!" Reggie
glared over the railing at his
prisoners.

In the fountain below sat Rataxes and Basil, looking very silly. Thinking quickly, Basil said to Babar, "Lord Rataxes has come to talk about a trade agreement to end the blockade."

Rataxes sat up straighter and tried to look kingly, while Basil explained the terms of the agreement. "Lord Rataxes will return your pomegranates and end the blockade on one condition: You must give us a thousand pounds of feathers."

"Agreed!" said Pompadour and Cornelius, before Babar could object.

The next morning, Rataxes sneaked into Celesteville wearing a long dress and a bonnet. Disguised as Lady Rataxes, he planned to trick Reggie into coming home with him and keep all the pomegranates besides!

"Here, Reggie! Come to Mama," called Rataxes. But he wasn't used to wearing high heels, and he tripped and fell flat. Reggie growled at him suspiciously, but Rataxes slipped the leash over his head.

Reggie tried to get away—and dragged Rataxes right through the great pile of feathers that the elephants had collected for the trade!

Again, Rataxes landed in the fountain—this time, covered with feathers. Every ostrich in the kingdom had contributed its feathers to the cause! Cornelius hurried out of the palace and said, "As you see, Lord Rataxes, we have your feathers ready."

"But these are *white* feathers," said Rataxes. "I wanted *fuchsia* feathers."

"No!" said Babar. "He's changing the deal!"

Pompadour tried to reason with Rataxes. "But Your Highness," he said, "think of all the baby elephants who are being deprived of their favorite fruit."

"And all the grandmother elephants who are pining for their pomegranate tea," added Cornelius.

But Rataxes wouldn't budge.

"No fuchsia feathers, no pomegranates," he declared. "I'll be back tomorrow." Holding the hem of his dress up out of the mud, Rataxes made a grand exit.

Pompadour and Cornelius were very upset. And they became even *more* upset when Reggie ran into the palace and scattered all the papers they had prepared for the trade agreement!

That evening, Cornelius
came to Babar and said
gravely, "Your Majesty, I think
it would be wise to find a new
home for your pet. I believe
your attachment to him is
interfering with our efforts to
solve the blockade problem."

"I'm not giving up Reggie, Cornelius," answered Babar. "And I'm not giving in to Rataxes."

But Rataxes and Basil had not given up, either. They had just slipped into the palace wearing suits of armor as protection against Reggie, whom they planned to kidnap.

The little warthog spotted his old enemy at once and raised the alarm.

35

Then Reggie chased Rataxes into the garden. There he tripped over the huge pile of feathers that had just been dyed fuchsia. Rataxes' suit of armor fell into a dozen pieces, and he roared with frustration. "Keep the feathers!" he shouted. "I want the warthog!"

Angrily, Babar answered, "It's not about warthogs, or fuchsia, *or* feathers! It's about bullies!"

At that moment, Rataxes was horrified to see his wife stomping into Babar's garden. "*There* you are!" she said to her husband angrily. "Why aren't you tearing down the jungle to find my Reggie?"

"Ummm, er, well, my dear...," said Rataxes, brushing off feathers. But before he could think of an excuse, Lady Rataxes spotted Reggie in Babar's arms.

"My little Reggie," she cried delightedly.

"*Your* Reggie?" asked Babar.

"Oh, yes, my dear," sighed Lady Rataxes. "I've been so unhappy since he ran away. But I see that you've taken wonderful care of him."

Reggie began to struggle toward Lady Rataxes. With a heavy heart, Babar handed him over.

"Ahem," said Cornelius. "Now about our pomegranates..."

"They will be returned to you at once," said Lady Rataxes firmly.

Rataxes simply nodded in agreement.

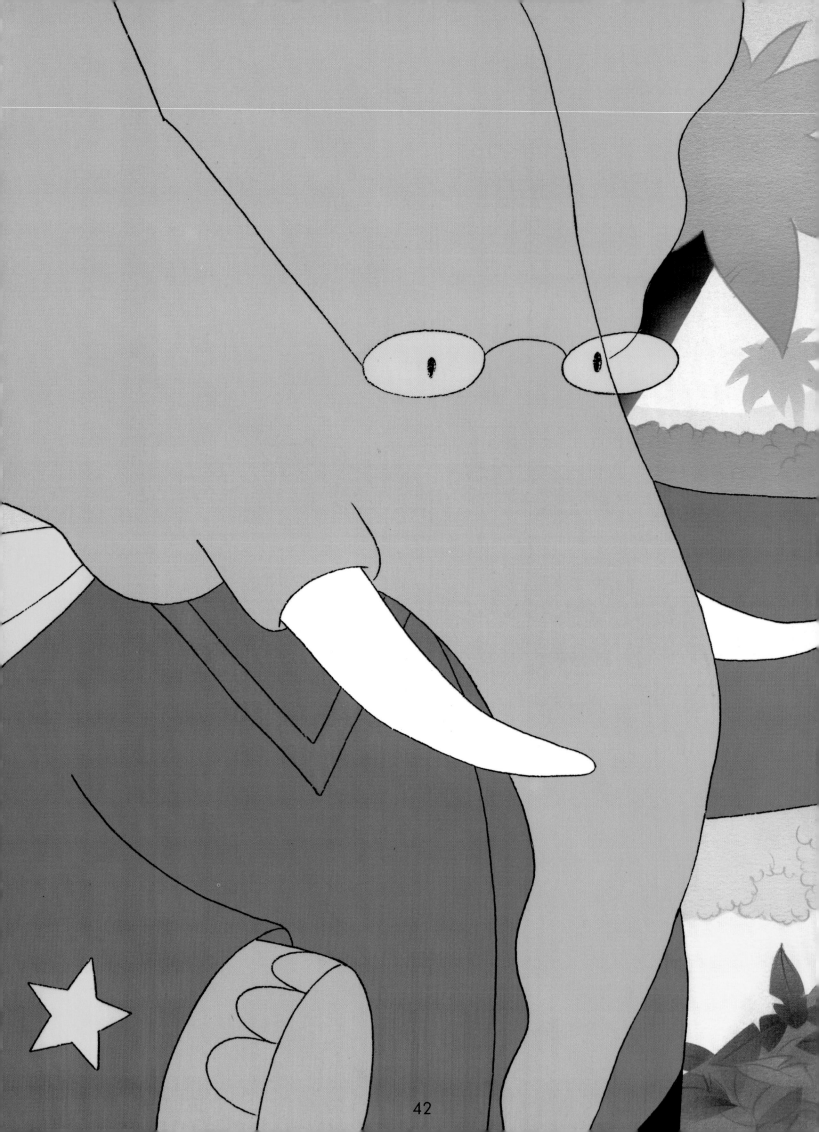

When the rhinoceroses had left, Cornelius turned to Babar, who was crying.

"That was a very brave thing to do, Babar," said the old general. "Thanks to you, Celesteville has her pomegranates, and, what's more important, her pride. I'm sorry it cost you a friend."

Babar was too overcome to speak.

...“Now,” said Babar, ending his story, “it seems to me that instead of spending time missing old friends, we can spend the time remembering how good it was to know them.”

Flora brushed away the tear on his cheek. “I love you, Papa,” she said.

Babar answered, “I love you, too, Flora.”